Cat and Fish

Illustrated by **Neil Curtis** Written by **Joan Grant**

Simply Read Books

One night, on his wanderings, cat met fish. They came from different worlds, but they liked each other's looks.

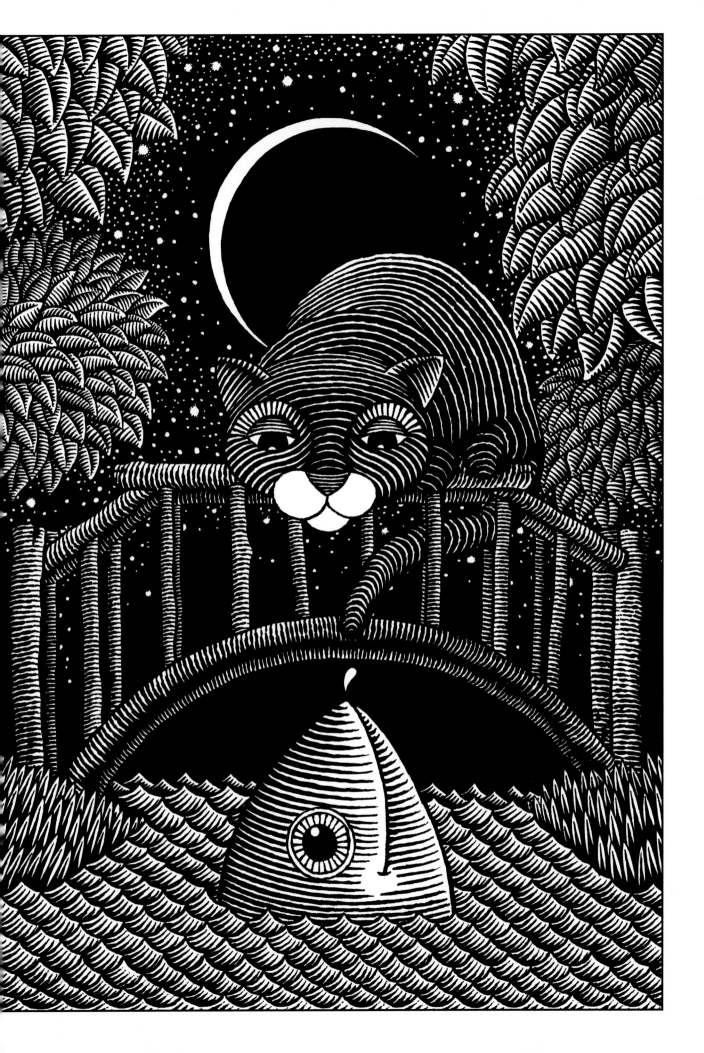

In the park by the lake they got to know each other. Fish told cat about the water and cat told fish about the woods.

They played in the maze. Fish lurked and cat prowled.

Late in the night they
sheltered from the rain

and as the sun was rising they stole away together.

Cat showed fish
his cosy hide-out.

He showed fish how to climb

and how to live on land
on cold nights.

But fish was lonely
for the water, so
cat found a boat
to take her there.

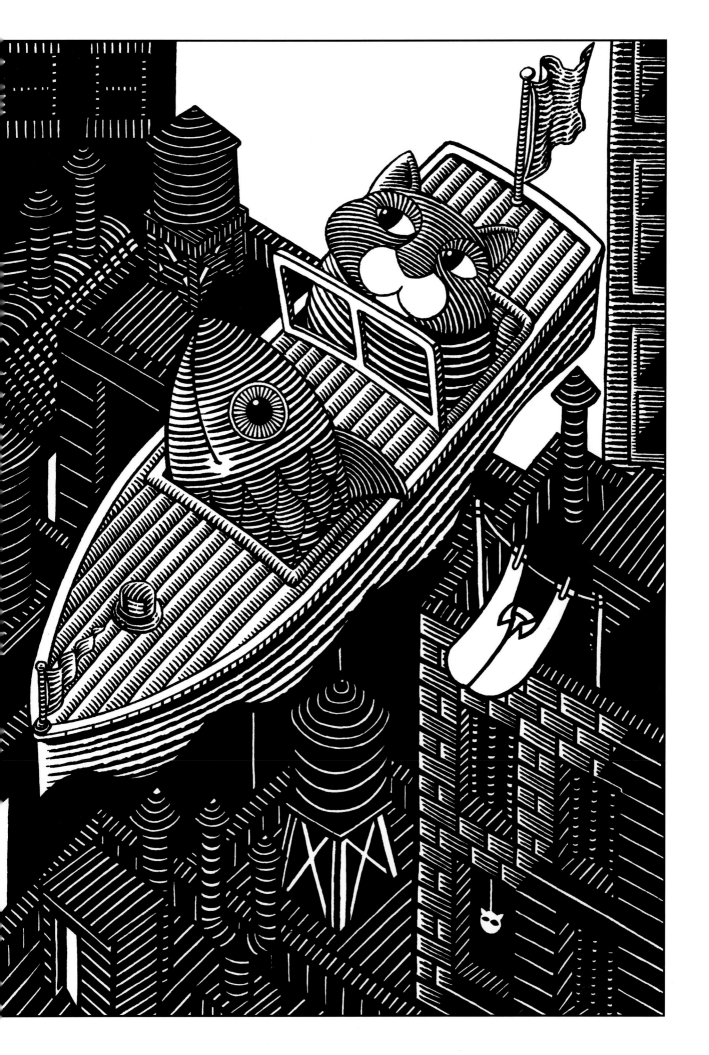

On the way they took
a wrong turn and went up
instead of down.

When they got there, cat
wasn't sure he liked the ocean.

But fish played and
cat found he could float.

And cat met fish's friends.

They decided to live where the sea and the land met ...

and rest until their next adventure.

For my mother, N.C.
For my grandchildren, J.G.

Published in 2005 by Simply Read Books Inc
www.simplyreadbooks.com

Illustrations © Neil Curtis 2005
Text © Joan Grant 2005

First published by Thomas C. Lothian Pty Ltd

Cataloguing in Publication data

Grant, Joan, 1931– .
  Cat and Fish/Joan Grant; illustrated by Neil Curtis.

ISBN 1-894965-14-0

I. Curtis, Neil, 1950– . II. Title.

PZ10.3.G77Ca2005   j813'.6   C2004-902816-2

10 9 8 7 6 5 4 3 2 1

Illustration medium: pen and ink
Design by Ranya Langenfelds
Film by Digital Imaging Group, Port Melbourne
Printed in Singapore by Imago Productions